POLAR SLUMBER

DENNIS ROCKHILL

Raven Tree Press

A Division of Delta Systems

www.raventreepress.com

POLAR SLUMBER

DENNIS ROCKHILL

To my very special snow angels Autumn, Holly and Sue

Rockhill, Dennis.

Polar slumber/by Dennis Rockhill—1st ed.—Green Bay, WI.
Raven Tree Press, a Division of Delta Systems c2006.

p. cm.

Audience: All ages

SUMMARY: A backyard snow bear becomes an integral part of a
little girl's slumber. She explores the arctic landscape in the bear's
company and awakens to question the authenticity of the experience.
Was her excursion fantasy or reality?
ISBN: 0-9741992-8-1

1. Snow (Polar bear)—Juvenile fiction. 2. Polar bear—Juvenile
fiction. 3. Dreams—Juvenile fiction. 4. Fantasy—Juvenile fiction.

2006933676
CIP on file.

Printed in China
10 9 8 7 6 5 4 3 2 1
First Edition

POLAR SLUMBER

DENNIS ROCKHILL

Raven Tree Press

A Division of Delta Systems

www.raventreepress.com

An early
moon turns
the white
snow blue.
A soft blanket
covers my
yard.

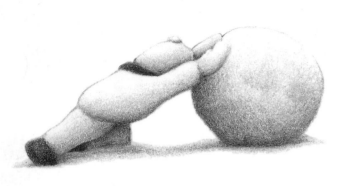

4

Frosty crystals
float and glide.
One kisses
my cheek.

7

Every flake
has its own
story to tell.
Each one
whispers
a verse.

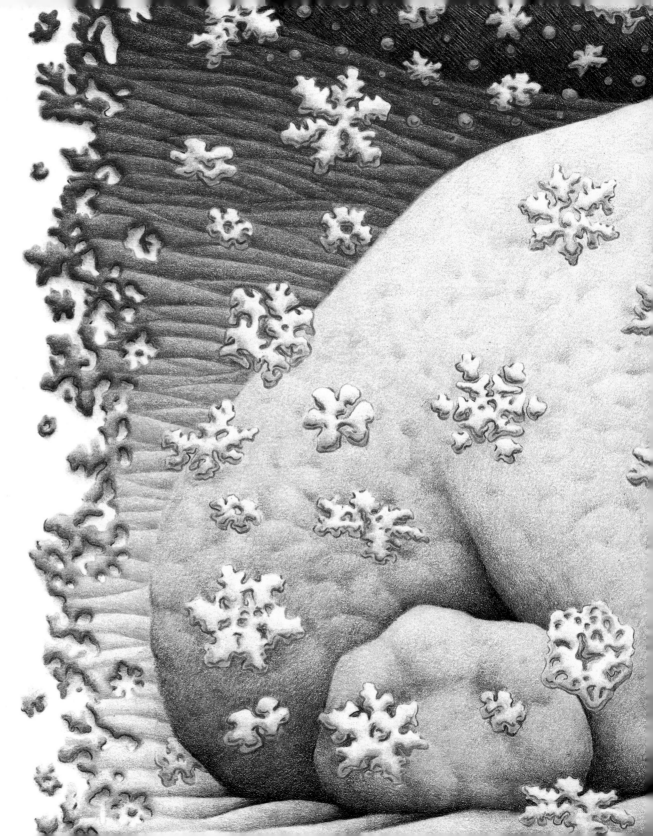

I close my
eyes and
listen to the
wind sing
a sleepy
lullaby.

11

Snowflake
dreams enter
my room.
A winter
wonderland
awaits.

14

Gentle,
furry friends
invite me
to join
them.

15

This is their
home.

We explore
the northern
beauty on
this moonlit
arctic journey.

Snow stars
fill the night.

We dance
and tumble
on a powdered
playground.

The
wind sings
quietly
as waves
of light
shimmer.

Our eyelids
grow heavy.
We snuggle
together...

27

in a
peaceful
polar
slumber.

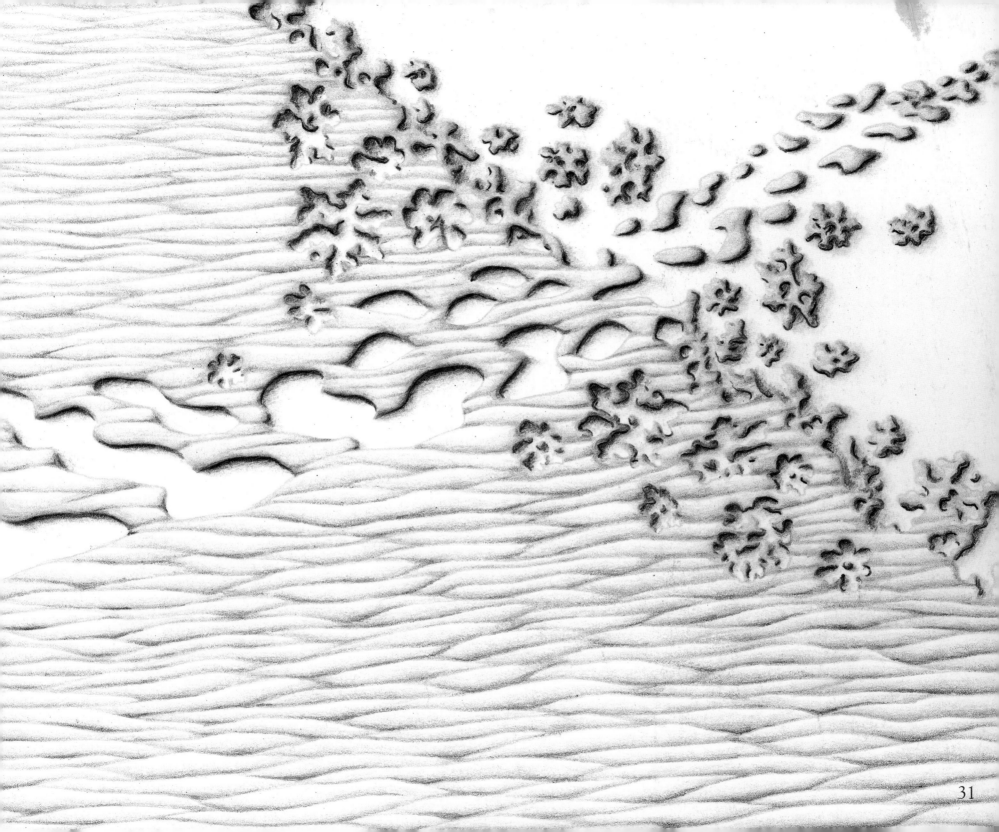

31